THIS HOUSE IS FILLED WITH CRACKS

poems by

Madelyn Camrud

Minnesota Voices Project Number 61

NEW RIVERS PRESS 1994

Copyright © 1994 by Madelyn Camrud
Library of Congress Catalog Card Number 93-83976
ISBN 0-89823-153-1
All Rights Reserved
Edited by Roger Blakely
Editorial Assistance by Paul J. Hintz
Cover by Madelyn Camrud
Book Design and Typesetting by Peregrine Publications

The publication of *This House Is Filled with Cracks* has been made possible by generous grants from the Dayton Hudson Foundation on behalf of Dayton's and Target Stores, the Jerome Foundation, the Metropolitan Regional Arts Council (from an appropriation by the Minnesota Legislature), the North Dakota Council on the Arts, the South Dakota Arts Council, and the James R. Thorpe Foundation.

Additional support has been provided by the General Mills Foundation, Land o' Lakes, Inc., Liberty State Bank, the McKnight Foundation, the Star Tribune/Cowles Media Company, the Tennant Company Foundation, and the contributing members of New Rivers Press. New Rivers Press is a member agency of United Arts.

New Rivers Press books are distributed by

The Talman Company
131 Spring Street, Suite 201 E-N
New York, NY 10012

This House Is Filled with Cracks has been manufactured in the United States of America for New Rivers Press, 420 N. 5th Street/Suite 910, Minneapolis, MN 55401. First Edition.

For mother and father

ACKNOWLEDGEMENTS

Some of the poems in *This House Is Filled with Cracks* originally appeared in *Loonfeather, The Nebraska Review, The Northern Review, North Dakota Quarterly,* and *Permafrost*.

"Walking on Cracks" was one of a group of poems to receive the Thomas McGrath Award sponsored by the American Academy of Poets.

"First Memory" © 1990 by Louise Gluck. From "Arafat" by Louise Gluck, published by The Ecco Press. Reprinted by permission.

I thank Jay Meek for his support when many of these poems were just beginning, and for his continuing support. I thank, as well, Roger Blakely for editing the manuscript, and the editor and staff of New Rivers Press. Special thanks to Evelyn Carlson, Barbara Crow, Janet Rex, and Donna Turner — members of *Other Voices*, our writers group — who continue to encourage the writing process, and to my husband, Ted, for his ongoing patience, understanding, and love.

CONTENTS

I.

II.

III.

IV.

I

*"In the dream, I am lying on my bed.
I look up at the ceiling and see that
some old cracks have reappeared."*

—Dream Journal

BEFORE RISING

My day starts by remembering other days,
     stacked in rows
like canned goods on basement shelves.
     In the farmhouse,
blue-tinted Ball jars colored peaches green—
sauces stored for winter above pickles,
     stewed tomatoes,
and string beans, cut by inches, packed in pints.
There was a washtub, galvanized, for baths
     near the sewer hole.
We used water, in turn—mine was soapy and cold.
I hid behind the furnace and toweled my body dry,
     clean for another week.

Cement, cold and moist, absorbed wastes—
darkness seeping from the edge of the hole,
     a urine smell.
The cistern, nearby. Once a mouse died inside.
"Water shortage," I was told, and we drank less
     for a while.

When the flood of 1950 backed the coulee
     through the sewer,
the water rose quickly like slop in the pail.
I swore I'd get away from potato peelings, egg shells,
     and coffee grounds
chucked in dishwater. In a dream, years later,
too ashamed to speak, I stood by the cistern
     holding napkins
and spoons, used and filthy, in a transparent bag.

Dad, in warm flannel, stood beside me and smiled.
His arm went around me as we walked upstairs.
    I wrote the dream
to remember how he whispered, "I love you."
    Today,
I take a notebook from my bedside table,
and fumble under its cover for a clean page.

THOSE OTHER WORLDS

Sometimes when I look at the moon I remember
coming home, summer Saturday nights. In the backseat
of the '41 Ford, I sat, having had my fill
of ice cream, maybe a movie — Fred MacMurray,
Claudette Colbert on a portable screen. Sometimes,
there was a magic show, women in mesh stockings,
a man with colored scarves that disappeared:
all of it in the town hall on Thompson's main street
where groceries were exchanged for cream and eggs.

The window of the car, like a crystal for gazing,
led to those universes, washed blue, where people
said real things, where they hugged as if they cared,
spoke loving words, and touched each other's faces.
In the moon, there were children who gave tears
like gifts, and told their mothers if they were scared.
Past the fields, vast as planets, there were
others who wondered about these things. Beyond the hum
of early insects in North Dakota, World War II,
I believed there were those, like myself, who wanted,
so badly, to reach farther, they almost met me halfway.

DAKOTA PASTURE

In the spring when calves burst onto rings
of steaming grass, I stood
in the pasture, knowing everything about living.
All that I wanted to do would surely happen.
Cows licked sacks and blood while the coulee overflowed
a dam of rocks piled to save it for summer.
Water gorged sod on its way to the Red,
flattening fences, filling ditches,
turning fields into mirrors losing their silver.
The smell of silage, fermented all winter,
grew rich in the hill-pit where cows gnawed
and chewed its thawed edges. One early Easter,

my sister went wading in the coulee,
icy water no higher than her knees.
Her hair, done for church, took the wind
in its curls; she was prettier than most,
her curves soft under a dress.
Pneumonia came in three days, gray cough
and high temperature nearly killing her.
She survived like the rest of us girls
with no brothers, with a father in the fields,
and a mother too busy to touch. One mile farther

past the mailbox, there were cousins
who had front zippers for peeing.
They taught us something about differences,
about being. In this pasture,
squared by ditches filled with water in spring,
where green took a hue of great intensity,
I saw it all in the absence of hugging and kissing,
always with no talk of love. Whirlpools form,
dipping and swirling, water falling over the rocks:
I go back to the edge of that wash-out where I stand
looking in, hoping for something to hold.

HANGING

I watch tree shadows playing against
the wall, moving in and out like leaves
under leaves, and I am reminded of all
that is temporary, the people whose lives
have faded into pictures. My grandparents
hang in a frame. Their sepia smiles

soft as the wind I hear outside. I know
my own time, its loneliness, brief
as the distance from the old blue spruce,
its branches blown close to my window,
and the kalanchoe that grows on a shelf
inside, thick with its bright, orange blooms.

IN THE MIRROR

Today, musty faces reappear. They are moaning
like my father, suffering more than they ought to,

before dying. I turn away, remembering dreams—
father's coffin in a room, his yellow body, a blue suit

with silk tie. He smiles when I enter and reaches
for me. "Why can't you die?" I say. I'm reliving

those dreams, nights when inside that dim room,
I turned away, afraid. If I had taken his hand

and found it warm, I might have gone on living,
and left the dying to him. Instead, I'm revisiting

old closets, stale dresses and lace handkerchiefs.
I visit the cemetery, fenced by Chinese elm:

Father lies here in his grave, his satin space,
like a trunk or a photograph, faded, misplaced,

in land where wind howls, dust smells. After summer,
I begin my lament, "Where are the dead?"

I return to the mirror and see chapters of leaves,
stacked one on the other into features. I am

flesh over bone in a hollow hall, rattling like talk,
tired of lying. I say nothing and forget to stop.

RED RIVER OF THE NORTH

Standing on my backyard hill I see for a year
and remember days, like trees. Some, in my mind,
are strong, though fallen piles lie deep on
the grass, a heap in my throat. The empty swing
with its weathered board rests on a knotted rope.
The river runs, people ride a boat, their laughter
floats from the deck. I watch, like the summer
I cannot stop. My children came at intervals,

happening one at a time, like seasons. I am home.
They have scattered and August shows its color,
an early fall: I care about leaves, the shadows
cast, the fluttering light shining through. I see
the past and I struggle like the river as it winds
to the north. Work keeps me alive, but my thoughts
tend to rise in rings of pain. I am trying to say,
"I have made mistakes. They are in my yard."

ANOTHER DAY

A bright morning. I walk past my neighbor's house.
He returned from Mayo Clinic last week, esophagus
gone. Eight-hour surgery gave him another chance.

I walk under the sun, I am just beginning to see
the day. Light moves, going in and out. I swallow,
walking faster. Shadows are everywhere, cast

from wire fences, and others from wooden poles.
Some follow cars. I see them fast as light;
I reach, they disappear like a cell burned out.

Now I am moving under trees, minutes passing
between the leaves. The day is not quite mine,
all that would have happened, has not. Over

the railroad track, I walk, the sidewalk covered,
woven wire. Trucks and cars driving by—an hour
has passed, the day is taking place. My neighbor

in his house still has a chance. I cast a shadow.
Over my shoulder, I see, the faster I walk, the faster
it moves behind me. And yet, I have not tried to stop.

DARK BIRDS

Dark birds, dark birds, like a storm descending,
swoop lower, as before. On my bed, I unfold,
a tired woman — blood dried, tears gone, tubes
and reservoirs, hollow bone. An ovarian moan
repeats, "I have given too much." Every moon
cycle has passed. I dreamed a girl pointed

a gun at me, could have pulled the trigger,
"But I love you," she said. Some find me dear
like a bureau or a chair — I shine, my old flesh
worn smooth. Each night I undress, my flesh
grows older — its tone less mellow than oak.
My mouth dries. The girl inside closes her eyes.

WASTED MORNING

This year white spaces are larger, covering
pages as if everything's been said. The lake,
full as ever, has less color—gray waves wash
its shore, end in foam. I've known for some time
I've let too much go—acres of sand pile higher,
deeper footprints go nowhere. My neighbor

has cancer that began in her ovary. Her eyes,
faded brown, tell me something about dying.
Each day pain takes more life from her face.
She waits on her dock, looking across the lake,
while I watch from my deck this fine summer day.
All morning my paper takes words I can't write.

BATHING: MY HUSBAND AND I

We make silence now, the quiet water
where we wade knee-deep, then deeper,
each in our separate directions.
There's a lake between us. Sun going down.
We come from water to sand, no reason
to talk about color, or water temperature.
Inside our cabin, voices flattened —
words, like dead friends, gone quiet.

This bathing is not the same as the rush
of our touching, the noise of flesh
washing flesh, when we make love.
We have nothing to say. If we could tread
the deep water, or swim, noisily, to shore,
we might forget the thirty years we've turned
gray together. In the false calm of this water,
this wavelessness, we stay, like a mood,

unchanged. We are living the fading we see
in each other. Who will pass first, like light
over water? Will the other be like a wave
washed ashore? He stirs in his chair, a book closes —
the silence, breaking in stages. We try too hard,
I'm not listening to him. Through the window,
I hear the marsh, the loud frogs like one
voice, drenching the dark with their song.

THANKSGIVING

The sky is the same. It's gray, and heavy
like November fallow, a field turned over,
just once. The day, like so many others,
in a season that hardly happens, passes —
somewhere between now and yesterday.
Thanksgiving goes away like all the days

I wait for, cold falling by hours, "before"
turning to "after." Other seasons were green.
On Orchard View Farm we raised apples and plums —
fruit stored in bins, used up by the years. Silence
grows in empty places. When I was six, my sisters
hitched a wild calf to a wagon, put me in and laughed.

"You're naive," big sister says, "always been."
Cold sharpens. It's crisp as the pleats
of a skirt I never quite got ironed straight.
We girls have grown. We're not that young,
anymore. Our father, whose birthday would have
been today, died twenty-three years ago.

Snow starts, small flakes dusting fields
and roads; some catches on stubble to become
a drift; some gathers in grass along the edges
of ditches. My sister settles in her chair.
She is larger than me, like a mother. We listen,
together, through the distance a day takes.

JUNE MORNING

There are mornings I don't want to rise,
mornings like this when I wake to the droning,

another plane spraying bugs or weeds. Across the river,
a farmer's field, under poison, yields a cloud

that drifts into my yard. It's that time of year.
I think of my neighbor who died last week

after one month of cancer. A block farther,
there's another in chemotherapy. I remember

when Dad's salivary gland developed a lump.
For potatoes, he sat like a rock on the tractor

waiting until dusk to spray. When the wind
was still, he pulled the cloud around him.

"I could taste it," he confessed to Mother.
A decade later, thin and frail, he turned

yellow as a potato left in the bin too long.
"It's cancer," he said, "not dying, I fear."

Long skeletal hours, he lay in his room — pain,
and groaning, until the coma came. In the morning,

he died. It was June. Today, I'm awake, like a leaf
or an insect, lying in the bed of my second story

room. I hear the spray-plane drone low as it comes
and goes, turning back to attack another row.

AUNT MAGANA

She breaks in bed, as easily as she is turned,
this Norwegian woman whose spotless kitchen
is an empty reflection back there on the farm.
A hollow body, under a sheet, she is propped
on a hospital bed. Rotting from inside out,
it is hardly a natural death. I remember

the yellow pantry, shades pulled in summer,
the lefse spots turning golden brown as I watched
from the round oak table. There were cousins
and sugar lumps, a Christmas tree. Her company;
her church. Stjørdalen's organist, forty-one years.
A memory: she touched my curls, that time,

when I stooped to admire moss roses in the sun.
They filled the space between her house
and sidewalk. Just beyond, in the center lawn,
stood the pump, painted white. Now her bones
are falling apart. Her smile is still the same.
We say good-bye, and she takes her hand from mine.

II

*"Roses, the snows of winter
still fill me with grief."*

— Daybook

NEARLY FALLING

I don't know when I first learned
that I crave pain, when I knew, somehow,
the dark curtain that draws my mind shut
has been hung by a yearning,
a desire to be sliced thin as threads.
Some part of me wants to show its blood —
I know this, just as I know that a fabric
torn loose from a garment takes on interest
in its edges. Out on the deck,

I lie back in my redwood chair
as if waiting for someone to strike me.
Suddenly I'm hit by a dream I recollect:
my right thigh has been sliced,
the deep cut separating layers of flesh
in cross-section like a river bank.
My fingers push the skin together,
but my heart wants to open it further.
All afternoon while I sit, there are cries

from a nest of downy woodpeckers
curled in the bark of a large ash tree.
Just when I find I'm nearly slipping
from my chair, when I almost let myself fall,
I hear their voices. And when I'm ready to hurl
my body against the wall, the sharp insistence
for life that rises from their throats
keeps me from crumbling,
like some useless old dress, to the ground.

ANGEL IN THE SNOWY FIELDS

*Brittany Eichelberger, a three year old
girl, wearing only underpants, was
revived after being found clinically dead
in a snowdrift . . . enchanted by the snow,
she ran outside to build a snowman for
her grandfather. "*

— Associated Press

In the backseat of the Ford, I'm an angel
in blue velvet, white-stockinged in garter belt,
going to church, Christmas Eve. Ribbons tying curls
either side of my head, I raise my face, gaze
through the window to stars, dazzling and white,
fluorescent snow. I want to run out
and be lost on those crystals under moonlight,
those mindless fields stretching left,

then right. In my heart, I hold the smell
of an uncle who'd held me close, buried my face
in his chest. He's the one I would have blessed
with a snowman that Christmas; for him,
I would have run out in the cold, unafraid,
nipples erect, arms outstretched, would have
fallen, would have listened for his call —
"Puds, Oh Pudsy! Where are you? Let me tickle
you, hear you giggle!" I would have
lain there on the snow, watching the stars
till he came and I rose, white and clean.

20

That night, as I recited my Christmas piece,
facing rows of broad shoulders in pews,
I was still running, headlong across the snow,
seeking the love I deserved, teasing, pleasing.
Tumbling and rolling, like an apple,
I made snowballs, stacking them till I fell
back, exhausted, to lie in sheer beauty,
fanning my arms, up and down, sprouting wings.

SUMMER PASTURE

I am walking, barefoot, by the coulee—
its muddy edge, cow-prints, and crayfish.
Mosquitos hum like the silence I sometimes
hear when alone in the house. Dark cattle
stand, knee-deep in the grass, stroking
tails. I am short, like my dress, showing
knee-scabs. The belt ties behind, under
buttons. My curls bounce. I am pretty,
and anxious, like a lover. My father
has not been home for days. Now he descends

the pasture hill in overalls, blackened
from work. We wade in the lush distance.
It disappears between us, his form rolls,
raises an arm, hand open. His face peels
back as if field-dirt gives him great joy.
White teeth shine through a voice, still
distant like a hawk-cry— "Hi, Puds."
The hand waves. I grin back as we cross
the purple of floating twilight, nearly touching.

THE WHITE ENAMELED CUPBOARDS
EDGED WITH BLACK

Whenever Mother leaves for the neighbors
or the store, not long after the Ford
has roared down the driveway, I go
to where the white enameled cupboards
meet the wall, and climb onto
the counter where I sit listening
to the clock tick. In a minute,
my hand slips naturally inside
the worn, cotton panties, and my fingers
find a place, unlike any in my house,
where there is feeling. Thighs spread,
I bend my knees to catch my feet against the edge
of the *Home Comfort* range. I sit,
pushing and rubbing as seriously as the cows
that graze their bellies back and forth
on box elders behind the barn, leaving the trunks
smooth and white in neat rows. Once, too,

perched just like this, I pushed and pulled
on my front teeth, loosening them long
before they ought to come out. When Mother
returned, she chided me—why do you want
to be toothless? I could not answer,
though I knew it was not for the joy of planting
those teeth, like two big seeds, in a glass
filled with water. I sat rocking
on the counter, blood and saliva spilled
from my gums, onto my tongue, falling
in tiny drops, like darkness,
onto my dress. I was a mistress,
of sorts, the way I was when Manley's hand

passed back and forth across my stomach
under my dress. Whenever I come
to this corner, and sit staring
at the clock, I cannot stop
till I hear wheels churning gravel
in the yard. When Mother's footsteps
hit the porch, I press my knees together,
remembering my shame the time she
caught me and called my fingers dirty.

DAD

I tried hard to entice
you, like the foxes you
went after with traps
or guns. But you turned,
seemed always to turn,
away and away, as you did
when I discovered your body
standing, large and naked,
in the washtub. That moment,

your hand slung out
for cover, organ hanging
like a carrot, the small wrinkles
wrapped round, you turned,
squawking like a hawk,
like those that turned,
away and away, filling
the air with their wings
days I walked in the fields.
                        That day,

as I stood on the cellar steps,
you turned, like a lover
afraid of loving, a father
ashamed, and the shame
rose to my face, reddening,
as I turned, running
like an animal, for cover.

CLOTHES WASH

At first, everything
in our house was done with care,
then later, with abuse.
The food we cooked, measure
by measure, swallowed like sorrow,
in a lump. Clothes,
like the stuff of our lives,
were taken in, then stacked into piles
for shelves and drawers.
Later, we tossed them
through the chute into the basement,
a tangled mass to sort again,
before washing. In my mind,

I go back, not by choice
but from compulsion to discover
something lovely in workshirts,
aprons, or socks, preserved
in patched overalls and underwear.
I bring clothes in from the line
and divide them, one more time,
into stacks. Later, I stand

on the cracked cellar floor,
soiled memories all around me,
and bend over, drawn
to the task of sorting
by color, separating dark
from light, soaking the stains,
scraping the grime, imagining
all the while another Monday's laundry
bleached, sudsed, rinsed,
wrung out and strung on the line.

IRONING

Those long summer afternoons,
in the turquoise, wainscoted porch, I stood
leaning over the board, steaming
the rickrack on Mother's aprons.
Drapes with peonies and broad leaves dressed
windows to the floor. I wanted to raise
a tall bottle, and swirl wine
down my throat, until I floated
into chasms where rivers rose
and fell, taking me in
the way a song fills
a mouth then leaves, breath
by breath. At times,

I wanted to go that far
to meet the man I imagined,
the one who resembled Jon,
but was far more attractive.
I gazed the half-mile to the mailbox
and pictured his lips sealing
a letter. Setting
the iron on its heel,
I went to the window and pressed
my lips against the frame's smooth,
pink, enamel. His arms closed
like warm darkness around me
as we kissed, then he ushered me
down a long hall and pushed me, gently,
to my knees. My body spilled
like milk onto a cushion
where we met, as if at the end of
or inside things, there was an answer.

HANDS

There was always a man,
a man's hands, never
a mother's, only

those fingers, lonely
and dark, like ink
spreading, taking me

for the pleasure of touching.
There was always that pleasure
not for me, but for him,

the way an organ gives
music when keys, dark
or light, are pressed.

MOON MIRRORS

I fall into my bed, ruffles folding
around me, summer nearly over.
I open my window to see the moon,
hear the wind washing trees: a cottonwood
by the river takes light in its leaves;
sound passes through
and comes back to me. I'm a woman,

easily lured, spending my life listening
to others who think they know better.
Tonight, once again, long shadows
like voices call me down to my fear.
Past my window, there are ghosts of old lovers,
always heard, never seen. Now I'm wiser,

all I need are memories: blankets spread under trees,
the boys I kissed who knew less about love
than I did. Going deeper, toward the river,
I enter sleep near the cottonwood:
its shimmering leaves, like mirrors,
where I see all the nights as a day, one single day,
                                        that I take
like a picture bathed in an incredible light.

KITCHEN

This is the kitchen, cast-iron pump
at the sink, a pail underneath

for catching slop. This is the kitchen,
linoleum spread with newspapers

after washing, black and white stories
we walked on, our soles twisting

them and tearing. Men coming in
from the barn after chores,

their overshoes staining clean pages.
We gather at the table, "Thank Thee

Lord Jesus, Amen," for potatoes and meat.
Saturday, bread dough set on the counter

to rise, some flattened for rolls, sugar,
cinnamon. This is the kitchen, one square room

to the north, a basement door, and newspapers,
those faces of women engaged to marry—

sheets laid on the floor, fresh at first,
all ripped and torn by Sunday morning.

SECRETS

It doesn't hurt me to tell
about Father, about
his leathery hands, how one took
mine into his palm as we walked
the streets of Thompson,
Saturday night. I ran along
the sidewalk, under streetlights,
fell on the graveled intersection
and scratched my knees to bleeding.
I can say with honesty, it was Dad's hands,
not Mother's, that gave me comfort.
It was he who seemed to love me,
his voice tender, mine at the edge

of tears. I can't as easily give answers
about the hand Dad hired, the one
we called Manley, who took me
riding on his motor bike. In the album
I see photos, he is standing
behind me, hands hanging
at this side. I remember his hands
best that time, sitting on his lap: his fingers,
long and soft, stroking my stomach
under my dress; his voice was soothing,
talking to Mother, busy
in the next room. Yet, in this poem
about hands, hired or otherwise,
I can say no more about the man Dad
hired to help him. I only know that today
I am still longing for my father,
as if, in truth, I never knew him,
never quite got enough of his hands.

III

"As Freezing persons, recollect the Snow —
First — Chill — then Stupor — then the letting go."

— Emily Dickinson
"After great pain, a formal feeling comes."

WALKING ON THE CRACKS

Tonight I am walking on the dim side of town
where police slowly cruise,
looking for cars stolen by children.
I'm wandering past houses that stand in close rows,
feeling like a prisoner of my own anger.
Like a hawk ready to swoop from the edge of a roof,
I want to leap into space and fly down,

talons spread. Tonight, I am deliberate
about walking on the cracks in the sidewalk.
Garbage lies on either side: styrofoam
and cellophane on the berm, bottles crashed
under hedges. Puddles gather mosquitos
in gravel driveways; the stench of summer
rises higher from leftover suppers.
I stop by broken steps where a door
left wide open echoes my craving to go inside
and find evil, not to tell it, but to live it,
as if the dirt never allowed in my house
could be smelled there. In the alley,

two men wearing T-shirts and brimmed caps
lean hard on a garage, lighting cigarettes.
Tonight, they're like bears,
like the one in the nightmares of mother
and grandmother that has lately been in mine:
he claws my screen door, finds the latch
carelessly open and comes in after me.

The men turn to walk as if looking
for something, elbows bent,
fingers curled, wild to hold what they catch.
Sweat shades their shirts like night shadows;
garbage cans dangle covers
from ropes in jammed racks. A cat cries —
raises its bristle like the blade
of a knife poised to strike.
I'd like to attack someone, too,
fighting back with my hands, until we fall,
screaming and clawing, like two animals
onto the ground, so that these secrets I carry
could be unleashed from my throat,
and my anger, like this seething desire
to find my darkness, might pass.

GRANDMOTHER

These words cannot talk about the quiet,
that long while you sat, arms folded
across your breasts, watching your daughter-in-law
working in your kitchen. These words,
so long after, cannot speak of the hopelessness
that kept you wrapped like a shawl
about yourself, those thirty years. These words

don't even come close to those that, likely,
filled your mind the day they drove
you into town—stopped at the nursing home,
walked you through that door, never
bringing you back, never bothering to ask
if you wanted to spend the rest of your life
in that room, tiled in brown and tan, that
green metal bed. How could a woman
who's crossed an ocean, left a family, and half
a heart back in Norway give up, as you did,
simply to sit on that stool, then step down
when they asked you. I cannot find

the angry answers you must have tucked
like your handkerchief, lace-edged,
in the pocket of your apron, never uttering
the disgust I saw only in the twist
of your hair, the long pins stuck through the bun
at the back of your neck. These words
are not the words you folded inside yourself—
those words sealed in your grave, changing
color, growing larger, there in the dark hollow
                              of your chest.

APPLES

He shouts at me from another room. Tears burn.
We've come around the circle again— the sink

still my place to turn. Apples spiral, peels
curling onto stainless steel, like the vows,

we renewed at our Silver Wedding— taking each other
for better, turning worse. Eight years gone.

My last daughter, no longer home. We've grown
older, turned away, too often, from anger.

He stays in his brown leather chair, under a lamp,
television remote-control in his hand. I stand

facing a wall, anger balled in stomach,
paring skin from the meat of apples I've picked.

My knife cuts to the core, spilling seeds,
quartering—it angles up and down, hacking apples

for baking. I pile slices into aluminum—leveling,
filling the pan to its rim. Dotting with butter,

sprinkling a cover of sugar and cinnamon, I conjure
an answer for him: "Let's eat it warm with cream."

VETERANS

Some days we live so desperately,
as if carving each moment,
like a name out of granite,
then running our fingers over the letters
to convince ourselves
we exist. In the center
of the dining room table, a bowl, hand blown,
holds the Star of Bethlehem: white flowers
creeping up the stalk, sucking
water, like a fetus,

through a stem. On the patio,
wind blows ceramic chimes strung
from a bell, notes tolled,
like old stories, through French windows
and doors. "Uncle Sarge," Mother says,
"is dying tonight": veteran of WWII,
he fought in Italy and Egypt;
stuck his neck out, took shrapnel,
came home with a purple heart.

                    Before bed,
I sit thinking of the Vietnam soldier
who died in the end
after struggling the length of the movie
to live. On this day,
this desperate day, I ordered bread
and a cake for Saturday's party;
tomorrow I've tickets for *Phantom of the Opera*.
In the morning I'll drive to work,
regulated, like the others: clocks
wound tightly toward war,
ticking closer to another. I'll drink

coffee from a cup, weighted
at its bottom to keep it
from spilling. By my own white-knuckled grip
I'll be turning, moving forward,
desperate in my struggle
to keep the black hands from springing.

DINING ROOM TABLE

Pressing graphite to paper, clean
through to wood, I practiced my name.
Perched on the hired man's lap, I sat
at the table, warm flannel of his breath
on my neck. Older, I pulled up close,
tucking my thighs underneath for whist
or rook, boy cousins, two big sisters,
laying cards where veneers came
to a center. All that winter

I was ten, Mother sat, pregnant,
at the table, holding her head
with one hand, working crosswords
with the other. Dad and I tuned
the radio loud to break the silence.
Big sisters, home for weekends,
spread newspapers on the table,
gave permanents and haircuts, scissors
nicking, scratching the surface. During the week

we stacked clutter, cleared it away
for Sunday eating. And each Thanksgiving,
lace draped over marred varnish,
we gathered, elbow to elbow, ravenous,
as soldiers just off bivouac—
Dad at the head, Mom at the foot,
the rest of us filling spaces
like teeth in a mouth, close, yet hardened
as enamel, one against the other.

DAD'S STORY

*"He would run a little ways and then
would stop, and look back in every
direction . . . He stopped quickly
when he saw me. I was pretty well
concealed and it took him a few seconds
to find out what he saw . . .
He certainly did know there was danger
in the air but could not locate it."*

—Milton Roeder,
"Still-Hunting The Fox,"
Hunter-Trader-Trapper (circa 1923).

Dad's story was lost by a household of women
he couldn't control
women who destroyed other possessions—
stuffed owl, crystal radio, glass-plate camera,
used for play. We toyed
with his maleness, three girls,
a young mother who didn't know any better;
we made fair game of the hunter
who tossed carcasses outside,
red bones lying in snow, frozen stiff.
He stretched pelts onto boards, fur-side in,
skin turned out, tails hanging, hides hung
and sold for coats. Somebody ought to know

the truth: two-by-fours cracked on rears
of spotted cows locked in stanchions.
Why would a man, at first gentle,
stab pitchforks into his cattle as if testing flanks
for doneness? He, the hunter in that barn,
scraped gutters, damned the cattle
while their tails switched. We daughters
and a mother kept house like bushy foxes,

clearing the table, breaking dishes,
destroying the story of a man
who was father. Afraid of
touching, we whispered questions:
Could a father ever make love with his daughter?
Would he, like an animal, do it outdoors?

Dad crawled in open country
behind snow drifts, seeking cover,
coming up against wind. Today,
on all fours, looking every direction,

I'm still rummaging in the attic.
Love eludes us, like the father,
under the cover of snow. He lures
victims from dens for attic-scent—
stacks of letters, browned edges, newspapers
clipped and torn—finding, losing,
losing, finding, we mistake others for him.

Father wrote of fever,
the attraction of a hunt, the satisfaction
of a shot that hits the mark. Daughters,
still running like little foxes,
looking back, listening, hear nothing,
coming into plain view of the hunter
who waits before firing the rifle
that could speak up and end the whole affair.

APPROACHING CHRISTMAS

I am walking across snow, measuring drifts
that take blue from light
cast just after sunset; a full moon
rises like a black hole, reversed,
in the East. Half a globe away,
soldiers, camouflaged,
spend hours hauling water:
breathing in, breathing out,
like swimmers. In the desert,
they wait, counting the days. At home,
we speculate about numbers of casualties.

　　　　Meanwhile,
my dreams these nights are of waiting:
a team of horses outside, bridled
and harnessed. With a sense of "not ready,"
I stand inside the barn, waiting for my husband
to come, to make love. Even in the dream
I think of oil lamps and virgins—
the five who filled their wicks, the five
who did not. Twelve years ago,
I dreamed of horses thrusting hooves
in bare earth, galloping
around a large grove of trees, all ablaze;
manes gleaming, they emerged
from a great sea of flame. Now the horses
stand waiting, harnessed and calm. How long
must I nurse my foolish passion
for waiting? When will I leave the barn
and take the reins? This evening,
as I walk, I look at the moon
and think of planting, of gardens
no longer in Babylon, and Saddam Hussein's

44

dream to restore them to glory.
The next minute, I recall
my own amazement, last year,
at first sight of Mother's breasts,
bared, a Venus of Willendorf
on the hospital bed. I imagined
myself pulling rivers of milk
through blue glands into my mouth,
my fingers pressing her sticky,
white flesh, in and out,
out and in. I knew then,
I wanted to take life, sucking it
clean through that nipple. Today,
on the other side of a war not yet begun,
life passes through me
to others. Walking like a soldier,
not quite ready to die, I wait
in the half of myself
not yet perceived, for the truth,
like the moon from its darkness, to unfold.

CALLED HOME

After sister telephoned, warned, "He'll never
last the night," we rushed home from fishing
and I walked into your room. Your hand raised
to take mine, almost like a kiss, intimate, sweet,
as we talked about walleye, and your eyes lit
with yearning to try, one more time, your hand
at fishing. I can still see you, so helpless,
lying in bed, glasses hanging on the end
of your nose. I turned to go when you called,
"Puds, I've something to show you." Then you

opened the drawer of the simple pine chest
beside your bed. Inside were booklets, stained
with grease, your name scribbled on each,
instructions for a combine, tractors, and a plow
you wanted me to keep, your own body worn
far beyond repair. I could see you trusted me:
"Keep them from Ma. She loses everything."
I answered, "Sure Dad," not really understanding,
not having a plan since not once did I go back
to that chest, not to that drawer, never again
did I look at those booklets, not those pages,
that, along with their machines, went at auction.

JUST AFTER EASTER

Had it not been that you died
the way you died—if you'd not taken months,
shelling off flesh; if you'd instead
been struck by lightning, or fallen, crushed
by a tractor, things might have been different.
If you'd not sweat through a coma,
mouth open, throat rattling, hands darting
across the blanket, sometimes passing
underneath to your penis as if protecting
that last bit of manhood—Dad, if you'd not,
that last morning, gasped for breath
like a rooster pulled, drowning,
from the stock tank; if it hadn't been
quite as it was, I wouldn't have felt

as if I killed you. If mother, my sisters,
and I hadn't kept such religious vigil
at your bedside that last night,
standing, watching you fight death,
we wouldn't have seemed so much like vultures,
noses twitching from cancer stench.
And that last morning, when I held down
your leg, flesh draped over bone,
muscles pulling, then stopping
to stiffen—if only then, I had let go
and stepped back to cry, I wouldn't
have gone on to live your death
these twelve years. Later,
when I grieved, I dreamed so clearly
of that morning: children climbing
through the window to the bedroom where you died,

like paper dolls of radiant color,
hand in hand, curling inside. Meanwhile,
bath towels hung on the clothesline:
cerulean blue, pink, yellow,
purple, a string of happiness from a childhood
I never knew. One by one, the children
tumbled through the window that June morning,
blatant as sin, as my denial that day
I'd passed you—dirty, in tattered jacket
and overalls, on the street—too ashamed
to speak. You never quite fit the picture
of the father I imagined. In the dream,
it was raining, towels flapping on the line.
I could almost see your face, tears
streaming in forgiveness as you flew
from that room, leaving us women—
the years of fear, simply standing there,
vacant, lifeless, a man no longer in the house.

LEAVING THE HOUSE

I close my eyes to smell
your sweat, to feel your flesh,
like moist clay, as if I must.
I think of you, eyes glazed over,
draped in white on that shiny metal cart,
and in my throat something catches,
not like fear, more like knots
lovers get, meeting in secret. I know now

just after you died, I walked out
to the morning, secretly glad,
feeling stronger. The way one falls
before the cross on Good Friday, even today
I am crying: "Let's get on
with this damned dying."
Outside there is sunlight, I've seen it
streaming through the cracks,
and I've imagined birds,
like ribbons loosed from a kite,
floating in the marvelous sky.

IV

*"I would pack if I could go with him. Unzip my skin
from by bones. . . . Leave thru the crack in the ceiling
where the soul passes."*

−Diane Glancy
"Portrait of a Lone Survivor"

FUNERAL: HOLMES CHURCH

Whenever I think of that drive, slow
down gravel roads, your body, drained
of blood, in the back of the hearse,
I never see you in white satin, the pleats
and puffs of that fabric, I see you, instead,
in the pasture, walking paths where cows
walked dripping milk, toward the barn.
Sometimes alone, sometimes like Jesus
on the way to Emmaus, friends walk with you,
those who knew you as a brother, some you hired
to fill the space of a son. Long before

we get to church, before we see the steeple
cross, the even white boards, before we slide
into a pew, clutching handkerchiefs, before we sing
"What a Friend We Have in Jesus," you've gone off
whistling in overalls and jacket, splotched
with grease, the way you did all those Sundays
we went to church without you. Long before
we march in pairs behind the coffin's flowery lid,
you've gone ahead, without saying a word,
to walk the pasture—land squared-off
and lasting, honest as good friendship,
with a coulee running through like a psalm.

JANUARY THAW

Elm and cottonwood line the path
along the river, branches sandwiched
in cold as if wrapped in cellophane
for storing and freezing. I imagine
river fish steeped in gloom,
their hearts as cold as gossip:
northern pike, catfish, carp, bullhead,
sauger, trapped until the dam gives way.
They wait, under ice,
milky eyes glazed and staring,
in the yellow-toned Red,
oxygen flows through their gills—a river in,
a river out. Suspended over a silken mud-bottom,
those fish accomplish silence,
like artifacts in a museum, displayed
under glass. Along the path,
an open pipe set in cement takes wind
as if all sound is contained
in one cylindrical note. I think
of this century rising then falling,

2001; my mind goes back to John the Baptist,
Peter and Matthew, those collectors of men
who drew fish in the sand as signs
of love and understanding. I hurry
toward home, remembering moments of my own,
stored carefully, growing colder,
fossilizing. Impatient for January
to lift its gray head, I envision
cold rising, like a fish from dank water,
taking sun in its scales—
each like the nail of a million different fingers,
transparent over flesh, reflecting

and gleaming—yellow, violet,
aquamarine. Shining back into water,
light swims: a single shaft
through the gloom and chill
that fall as residue to the bottom.
The brilliance continues, flicking
color, finning this way and that,
boldly as the sun, from the river
to the shore of one ocean, then another.

TRAVELING

Driving fast
down a gravel road
at twilight, I've lost
my direction, and turn back
to taste dust, hanging
low in the orange glow. This evening,

clouds slide, like decades
of my life, past
the horizon. Yet, even
as this century spins away,
the sky is still the sky,
an endless wash of grace that stays
and stays and stays.

SKINNY-DIPPING

It wasn't because I did it alone
made it delicious, nor because
walking into inky water
made me think of Virginia Woolf.
A streak of moonlight licked the lake
like the beam from the lighthouse
Woolf rowed toward with her father.

Stopping, listening to drops fall
from my hands, I thought
about Woolf, rocks in pockets,
sinking till she stopped
in the darkness. I'd waited
and, when the family was asleep,
taken such pleasure, on tiptoe,
in stealing from the cabin to the beach.
By the Adirondack chair, I let my robe slip,
white and plush, onto the sand. And cautiously,

I stepped into Grace Lake
stone-naked. Deeper and deeper
I walked, to my chin,
then stroked out along the edge
of the moonbeam, arms glazed and flashing,
cupping the water to my breast—
going down, coming up, head wet
and gleaming, then floating
back through black water. I crossed
the sand, in my white robe,
bare feet. Sliding between the sheets,
beside my husband, still asleep,
I smiled glossed with the ecstasy
of knowing the secret I would keep.

FLOATING ON GRACE LAKE

On my back,
gliding through water,
I'm like silk pulling silk.
My arms are wings spreading
reflections of clouds
until the sky clears. I imagine

I'm playing softball
with the Holmes team.
The ball I hit
makes no sound, it goes farther
and farther,
beyond the sky's blue leather.

IN THE ABSENCE OF LAND

Water bursting from cracks
in rocks, birthing,

once more, like *fossen*
rushing from Norway's mountain.

Running, always running,
we are women, faces opening,

then closing, like waves taking,
letting go: Randi from Marit,

and all the others before her;
Randi to Mali, then Mali

to Martina. In a long stream,
Mother, I'm coming, stroking

north till I mouth into the ocean—
that circle, deep and green,

a daughter made to become
another mother, another daughter.

CARRYING THE CHILD

I remember I'd no sense of the gift:
the child I carried inside me was something
I didn't know, no more than my extension—
a part of my abdomen that gave me indigestion.
Mother's test was simple enough:
carried up-front and high, it was girl;
wide and low, it was a boy—
she was right twice of my four.
Others dangled a needle from a thread
held over my wrist like a plumb line;
if it went across and back,
or up and down, it made a difference.
I don't remember which was which.

                                  What I remember,
is that my stomach stretched like a sail,
full-blown, to hold those limbs,
fists and feet that pushed deep into my pelvis.
I remember, too, how clumsily I rose from my chair,
the way my legs spread for balance
when I descended the stairs or tied my shoes.
Mostly, I remember the ignorance of my youth,
the way I denied the overwhelming,
by the simple act of living, all the while,
letting go of the miracle so it could happen.

CLEANING HOUSE

The morning sun sifts
through blinds into the room,
lighting the harsh edge
of a vase, warming
the bisque, ocher to rouge.
Stopping my chores,
I pause to look,

just as the last motor
of the house stops
and the ticking of the clock
on the mantle takes over. I think
of Grandfather, a gentle man,
walking a furrow
behind a plow drawn by horses.
Somehow I sense
in the moment the single cell
I once was, and those

millions I've become,
joining now, diffusing,
inside me. I hear
the thumping of my own heart,
like a sun ringing out.

SIGHTING THE MOOSE

We hadn't expected to see the moose,
not on farmland, and not then, when my husband
had just said, "I'd like to go hunting again."
Cattails rustled, and from the dry coulee bed
the moose rose, silent and ancient,
like my desire to find darkness,
that place where a scent or a sound
takes on brilliance. We stood
captured like lovers in a tryst, enamored,
at first, by his stunning nakedness.
                                   It was then,

I thought of caves, "The Hall of Bulls"
at Lascaux: mammoth, horse, bison,
boar drawn in red and yellow ocher
on the walls; hunters practiced, painting
arrows through bellies, throwing spears
as they danced, hacking the rock,
breaking the silence. In the dim light
of stone lamps, a wick of moss burning marrow,
I was struck by the magic—not of killing,
but of seeing. Just then, I sensed an urgency
to hold that moose in his pose, but he turned,
scaled the coulee bank, and ran
across the field. My husband stood beside me,
brave as all men, as afraid. I raised
my hand to shade my eyes, and watched that moose
grow, large as myth, just as his rack
                          disappeared over the ridge.

LIVING ROOM

I switch on that first lamp
and its light leads me to another,
the way one lost in a forest
follows a string to find her way.
Flicking switches and pulling chains,
as if knowing depends solely on seeing,
I shed light on this room where I've been
living so long, the worn chairs, a couch,
intimate as the eyes of an old friend
who smiles, no need to ask,
no need to doubt. My eyes

sweep the walls, shelves with books,
objects placed with great care.
I never wonder at the outlets
and cords, already plugged,
nor at the fact that I was led
into this room, stumbling at first,
like a child just learning to speak,
nor do I marvel at how that first light
leads me straight to another,
then another, till the room swims
like a fish coming up from water, flashing
its fins in bright sunlight, and I stand
in my living room, familiar, yet brand-new,
seeing it all for the moment,
                              taking it in.

TURNING CALENDAR PICTURES

Last night was like those nights
I climbed trees behind the barn
to reach leghorn pullets at roost
in the moonlight. To the henhouse,
we took them for winter nesting.
The moon last night had the same blue mold.
Wearing plain and wool, we did the gathering-in—
apples for storing over in the cold room
downstairs. My husband climbed the ladder,
I stood behind, steadying it; we shook loose
McIntosh we couldn't reach. Today, I understand

a little better the child who climbed—
scratching knees, chubby hands pulling her higher
than she dared. By December,
those pullets dropped eggs. Every day,
we searched their nests to find our breakfast.
This morning the river glosses under fog;
soon there'll be ice to walk across. Each year,

we manage to get ahead of the weather—
apples in the bin, potatoes, squash,
everything in its place as if stored all along.
Today, I'm grateful for the rhythm
of apples and eggs, glad the way my life unfolds,
starts again. The only difference
I notice is my skin; like a cracked cellar
                            it takes in more cold.

WATCHING

We know all about time now,
how it speeds, how it slows,

the way that one season closes,
then opens to another, the days

a ball of twine growing larger
on the prairie. We know

about moments like this, when
my husband and I put bird seed

in the feeder, then sit, side
by side, at a table to watch,

feeling as serene as we have
in any church. We bear

resemblance, in this small act,
to acceptance, perhaps forgiving

what we know of each other,
of growing older. The birds

know our shadows well, yet
they flutter, diving in and out

so quickly from the window,
not yet trusting as we trust

the mercies of bread crumbs and seeds.

IN THE ATTIC

Ribbons and beads spill
from my dresses, cast into a trunk,
the lid left open. I see colors,
crumpled and faded, the frayed edges
of satin, overused.
Sunlight streams through dust,
the way a mind sifts the past, sorts out
what it wants, then takes me back
till my hand finds the nape
of your neck, and we slow dance
under rafters, in the attic
of my house, dancing back the years:
lights dimmed, your lips warm,
hand hot on my back, our bodies
finding each other's hearts, lungs,
all organs like pipes breathing,
every step you take, an effort
to enter me. Then we twirl
through the sun's rays, and I see
that we are shadows, returned
merely for haunting, dancing, dancing,
long after the music has stopped. Sometimes,

I want to take life from the top,
one more time, like a choir
rehearsing, to make it perfect.
I might begin with the prom dress,
lavender taffeta, nylon net,
and, after swallowing that first kiss,
try harder to hold my tongue.
If my wedding dress had been creamy white,
instead of black, I might have stored it,
like love, and opened it now

for a look. I see black ghosts, instead,
like the bats in my neighbor's cabin, hanging
from the rafters, their droppings
oozing through the ceiling.
They nest among spiders, the webs
criss-crossed, back and forth,
strung from the ceiling
to the walls. They moan like wind
in the trees, their voices rising,
then repeating the way a tape plays,
rewinds, like a longing
for a lover, or the flowers
I never carried, the aisle I never
walked on Father's arm. Once, I dreamed

of roses, fresh and pink, springing up
in fine ashes along the bank
of a river. Today, I wonder at the loves
that burned my heart, those of my daughters
and my mother, at what we've lost,
what we've stored. I still grieve
for the loveliness of sins
pressed in old dresses, stored
in folds, or those hollows where breasts
once rose and fell. I recall
with sadness the passion
that passed through my groin, my daughter
fresh as grief, complete as joy,
on my breast. The past leaves

me empty, a dress, still warm
from a body, dropped onto the floor.
I live with ghosts in my house,
they stay in my attic like the stale odor
of a mouse dead in the walls.
I see them in nightmares, shadows creeping
down the stairs, like secrets
I don't know, those I've been told
to keep, and can no longer
remember. I try to climb the stairs,
never quite prepared to face them, like fear,
and make them go away. I want to tear
them all apart, like those old dresses
in my trunk, ripping seams,
gleaning threads, sorting them for moments
worth remembering. Those I'll handle

with care, as if they were velvet, trimming them
with a scissors like the tiny one in my dream:
handles and blades of aged brass,
an ancient gift taken from a wound.
I'll cast the scraps aside,
letting them fly through the window,
like brides loosed from a tower,
veils afloat like the seed of cottonwood
in spring. Others will fall
to the floor, worn to show its true grain.
Those I'll gather again, saying
"This is how it was," then stitch them
all together, no matter
what direction, on a backing of satin,
before I lay them on my bed
and fall asleep under the leaf
of one great crazy quilt.

". . . in childhood, I thought
that pain meant
I was not loved.
It meant I loved."

—Louise Glück
"First Memory"

Madelyn Camrud was raised on a farm near Grand Forks, North Dakota, and has lived in Grand Forks for all but two years of her married life. She received her B.A. degree in visual arts and English in 1988, an M.A. in English in 1990, and began working at the North Dakota Museum of Art in 1991, where she is the Director of Audience Development. She is one of the founders of the writer's group, *Other Voices*, which meets bi-monthly around her dining room table. Camrud and her husband have two sons and two daughters.

About her writing, she says: "Around fifteen years ago, someone told me to 'write it down.' I've been 'writing it down' ever since, and the 'writing' often evolves into a poem. What do I like about writing, especially poems? It's playful and fun, like a game of Scrabble, yet it's hard work. But it's the fact that poems allow me to look up, down, and crosswise at life that really appeals to me. I don't just *like* writing poems, I *need* to write poems."